ALI BABA

ALI BABA

Long ago in Persia, there lived two brothers, Ali Baba and Kasim. Kasim was a rich man but Ali Baba was poor. He made a living by selling the wood that he gathered from a nearby forest.

One day while Ali Baba was in the forest, he saw a group of men.

He was afraid and climbed a tree. "I will hide so that I can find out who these men are," decided Ali Baba. He looked hard at the men on horseback. There were forty of them. They tied their horses to the trees and began unloading heavy sacks.

"They must be thieves," thought Ali Baba.

Suddenly, the leader of the group stepped in front of a nearby rock and said, "Open Sesame!" Immediately, a rock magically opened to reveal a cave. All the thieves went inside and the rock slid back into its place.

After sometime, the thieves came out of the cave. The leader of the thieves shouted, "Close Sesame!" and the rock closed the entrance to the cave. The thieves rode away on their horses.

Ali Baba was curious. He climbed down from the tree and said, "Open Sesame!" in front of the cave. Once again, the rock slid away to reveal the entrance to the cave.

Ali Baba was surprised to see bags full of gold and silver inside the cave. He took two bags of gold home, and told everything to his wife. He told her to keep the secret while he went to bury the gold.

"Let me measure it first," she said. "I will borrow the scales from someone.

She ran across to Kasim's wife and borrowed her scales. Since Ali Baba was poor, Kasim's wife was curious to know what Ali Baba wanted to weigh. She put some glue on the scales.

Ali Baba's wife weighed the gold without noticing that a gold coin was stuck to the scales. Later, Kasim asked Ali Baba about the gold. Ali Baba told him the secret and so Kasim went to the cave.

Kasim was surprised to see so much treasure inside. He stuffed a lot of gold in his bag and turned to open the door. But he had forgotten the magical words and could not open the cave door. When the thieves returned to their cave, they saw Kasim and killed him. They cut his body and left it inside the cave in order to frighten anyone who already knew about their secret.

That night, when Kasim did not return, his wife told Ali Baba where her husband had gone. Ali Baba hurried to the cave and found his brother dead. He brought his body home.

A clever slave girl Morgiana lived with Ali Baba. She knew an old tailor Mustafa who was an expert in stitching. She offered him some gold coins for stitching a dead body and led him to Ali Baba's house with a blindfold over his eyes. There, he stitched the pieces of Kasim's body back together.

When the thieves returned to the cave, they found Kasim's body missing. "There is someone else who knows the secret of our cave," said the leader to his men. "Go and find that person."

Soon one of the thieves found Mustafa and came to know that it was Ali Baba who knew their secret. He marked the door of Ali Baba's house with a cross so that when he came back, he would be able to recognise the house.

Morgiana noticed the cross and made similar marks on the doors of other houses too. At night, when the thieves returned, they could not identify the correct house and left angrily.

The leader now disguised himself as an oil seller and reached Ali Baba's house with forty oil jars. The other thieves were hiding inside these jars.

That night, Morgiana heard the leader of the thieves discussing his plan to kill Ali Baba. Later in the night, Morgiana killed all the thieves in their jars by pouring hot, boiling oil on them.

When the leader arrived for dinner, Morgiana performed a sword dance and killed him with her sword.

Ali Baba was grateful to Morgiana for saving his life, and rewarded her by marrying her to his son.

Ali Baba sees forty thieves ride into the forest. "Open Sesame!" says the leader of thieves to a rock, magically opening it to reveal a cave. After they ride away, Ali Baba enters the cave. What does he find there?

Om Books International

Reprinted in 2022

Corporate & Editorial Office
A-12, Sector 64, Noida 201 301,
Uttar Pradesh, India
Phone: +91 120 477 4100
Email: editorial@ombooks.com
Website: www.ombooksinternational.com

Sales Office
107, Ansari Road, Darya Ganj,
New Delhi 110 002, India
Phone: +91 11 4000 9000
Email: sales@ombooks.com
Website: www.ombooks.com

ISBN: 978-93-52760-12-1

Printed in India

10 9 8 7 6 5 4 3 2

eBOOK available

ISBN 978-93-5276-012-1 US $ 3.99 £ 2.99
9 789352 760121
www.ombooksinternational.com
001250

Om KIDZ

ombooksinternationalofficial
ombooksinternational
ombooksdelhi